*This Golden Book belongs to*

_____

_____

# My Hanukkah Alphabet

## Photos by Claudia Kunin

**A GOLDEN BOOK · NEW YORK**

Western Publishing Company, Inc., Racine, Wisconsin 53404
Packaged by the RGA Publishing Group, Inc.

# Aa applesauce

**Applesauce** is a special treat during Hanukkah. Yum-yum!

# Bb book

Mommy reads me a **book** that tells the story of Hanukkah.

# Cc candles

We light **candles** on Hanukkah. Hanukkah is called the Festival of Lights.

# Dd dreidel

My **dreidel** spins just like a top. It will stop on one of the letters. Which letter will it be?

# Ee eight

We celebrate Hanukkah for **eight** days.

# Ff family

My mommy, my daddy, and I are a **family**. On Hanukkah, we give each other presents.

# Gg gelt

Grandpa gave me a bag of chocolate money called **gelt**—and a great big kiss!

# Hh Hebrew

The **Hebrew** alphabet is called the *alefbet*.

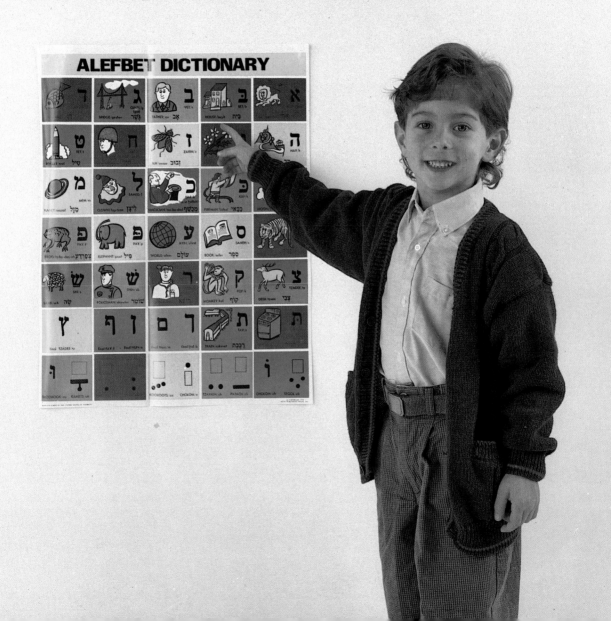

# Ii Israel

**Israel** is the homeland of the Jewish people. The Israeli flag is blue and white.

# Jj Judah Maccabee

**Judah Maccabee** was a brave soldier who helped to free the Jews a long time ago.

# Kk kiddush cup

During Hanukkah, Daddy says a prayer over the wine.
I drink grape juice from my very own **kiddush cup**.

# Ll latkes

**Latkes** are delicious potato pancakes that we eat during Hanukkah.

# Mm menorah

A **menorah** is a candle holder. A Hanukkah menorah holds nine candles. We light the candles from left to right.

# Nn night

We light one of the candles each **night** of Hanukkah.

# Oo oil

In a temple long ago, there was **oil** that lasted for eight days. This is one of the miracles of Hanukkah.

# Pp presents

I get eight **presents** on Hanukkah—one for each night.

# Qq quilt

Grandma made me a special Hanukkah **quilt**. It keeps me warm on cold December nights.

# Rr rabbi

A **rabbi** is a teacher. Our rabbi taught us that the word Hanukkah means "dedication."

# Ss shammash

The **shammash** is the special helper candle. It lights the other eight candles in the menorah.

# Tt temple

On Hanukkah, we go to **temple**, just like we do on other Jewish holidays.

# Uu umbrella

Sometimes it snows during Hanukkah. Then I go outside with an **umbrella**.

# Vv vest

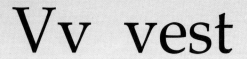

On special holidays like Hanukkah, I dress up in my **vest**.

# Ww words

The letters on the dreidel stand for the **words** "A great miracle happened here."

# Xx  xylophone

One of my Hanukkah presents was a **xylophone**!

# Yy yarmulke

Daddy and I wear our **yarmulkes** when we say the blessing over the Hanukkah candles.

# Zz zebra

On the last night of Hanukkah, my present was a brand-new **zebra**. Happy Hanukkah to me!